Alastair G Mckenna
Little Mermaid Sisters
The Magic of Fluffies

Copyright 2024 Alastair G Mckenna

First Edition Book, 2024

Book cover design, illustration, editing, and interior layout by:

www.1000storybooks.com

Dedication

This Book is for Donya

"Aleena," Miette said. "Aren't you excited? School starts tomorrow! I can't wait to see all my friends and try out the brand-new seesaw!"

Miette expected her sister to be as excited as she was. After all, Aleena had been asking when she could start school for as long as Miette remembered.

But instead of agreement, she heard the snorted sounds of Aleena's loud sobs.

Concerned, Miette swam toward her little sister.
"What's wrong?" she asked. "Would a hug help?"

Aleena nodded, and Miette wrapped her arms around her little sister. When the snorts and sobs stopped, Miette asked, "Do you want to talk about it?"

"It's just . . . I've never been to school before," Aleena said. "I have no friends there. I don't know anyone!"

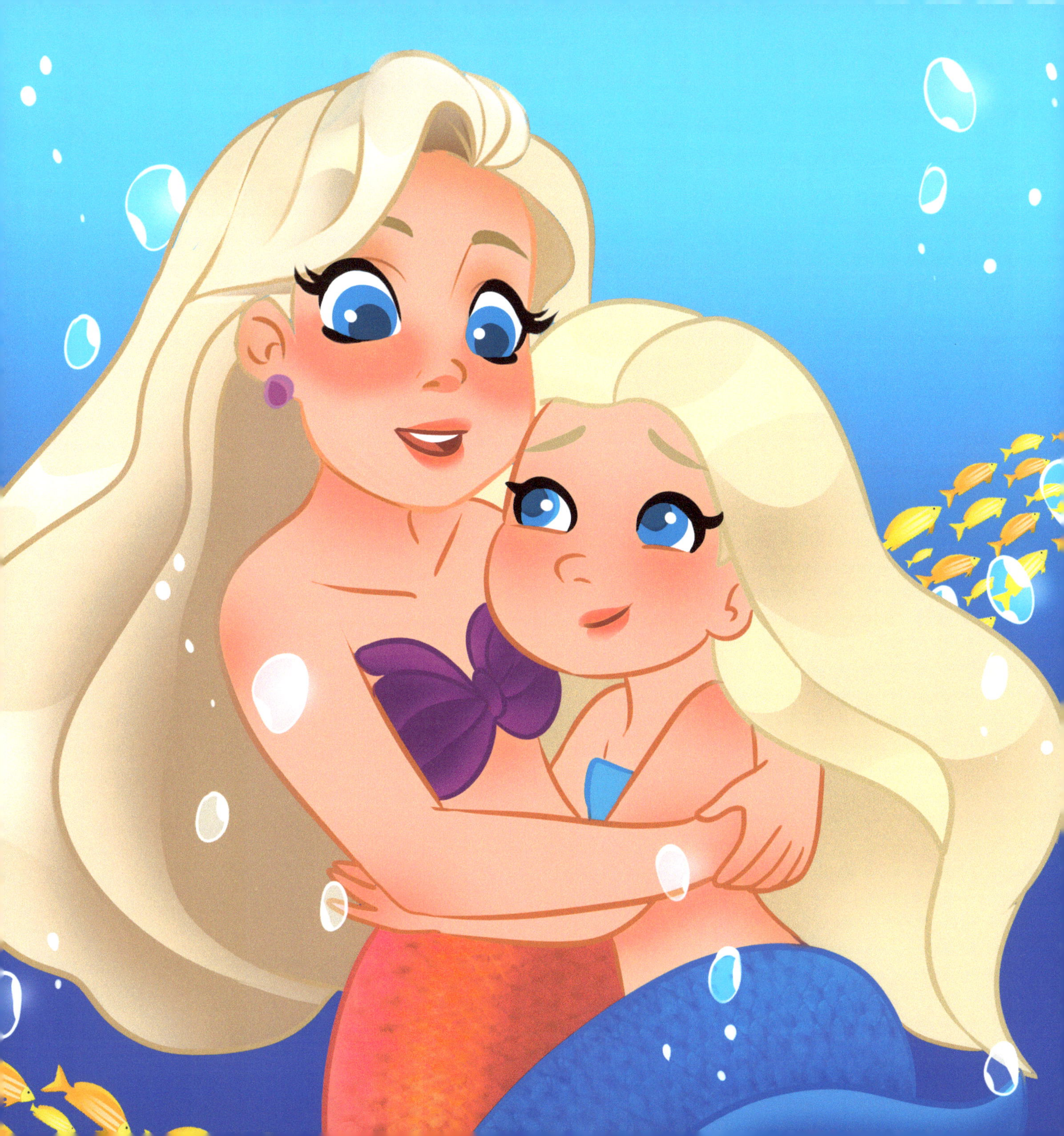

Miette listened as her sister spilled out her worries. Then, with a nod of her head, she said, "I know just what you need!" and swam off.

"Wait, Miette! Where are you going?" Aleena protested.

"Don't worry," Miette said, swishing her tail. "I'll be right back."

A minute later, Miette swam back, arms wrapped around her most special fluffies.

"Mum gave these to me on my first day of school," Miette explained. "She told me they would keep me safe, and she was right."

"Keep you safe?" Aleena asked. "How can they help? They're just fluffies!"

Miette grinned. "Because they're magic!"

Aleena tilted her head to one side, and a little smile started forming on her lips. "Magic?" she asked.

Miette nodded and handed a fluffy dolphin to Aleena. "Danny the Dolphin is fast and strong. Whenever you feel scared or upset, just hold him tight and he'll give you courage."

Next, Miette handed her sister a fluffy whale.
"Wally the Whale is silly and always makes me giggle."

"Oli the Octopus is a great way to make friends, because he holds up to eight things, like extra pencils, in his bendy arms."

"Sea Horse is always loving and kind, and he will remind you of how big your heart is."

"Uni the Unicorn is full of magic and will fill your imagination with beautiful thoughts."

"Are they all magic?" Aleena asked.

"Yes," Miette said, "but to release the magic you have to sing their song:

"I hold my fluffies near and tight

Then all day long, I'll be all right.

My Guardian Angels by my side,

In school today, they'll be my guide."

"I feel better already!" said Aleena

"See, they really are magic!" Miette said. "Now let's get our beauty sleep."

The next morning, Miette and Aleena were wearing the new coats and hats Grandma and Grandpa had given them for the start of school. Holding hands, they both got on the whale shark bus to Mermaid School.

"This is where you line up," Miette explained when they reached the school. "Look, here is your class, and your teacher!"

Leaving Aleena in line, Miette swam off to join her own class. Aleena took out one of her fluffies from her bag and sang quietly,

"I hold my fluffies near and tight

Then all day long, I'll be all right.

My Guardian Angels by my side,

In school today, they'll be my guide."

"Oh, cool!" said a mermaid standing behind Aleena. "I was really nervous, but that song made me feel better."

"Me too!" Aleena replied. "I'm Aleena, by the way."

"I'm Katie," said the mermaid. "It's nice to meet you, Aleena."

The two new mermaid friends smiled at each other as their teacher led them into school.

Later that day, after the morning lessons, the school bell rang for playtime.

In the corner of the playground, Aleena saw her big sister, Miette, with her arms folded, her head down, and her mouth to one side.

"Is everything okay?" Aleena asked.

"It's nothing!" said Miette sharply.

Miette's best friend, Elsa, joined them.

"Why is Miette upset?" asked Aleena.

"Your sister was talking too much in class, so the teacher made Miette move seats and sit on her own," Elsa explained.

Hearing this, Miette narrowed her eyes and pursed her lips angrily.

Seeing how upset her big sister was, Aleena knew exactly what to do. She swam up to her big sister, wrapped her arms around her, and said,

"I hold my sister near and tight

And all day long we'll be all right

With Guardian Angels by our side,

In school today, they'll be our guide."

Miette smiled and looked down at her sister. She squeezed her back, and the sisters started to giggle and laugh. "Let's play tag," Aleena said. "I'm it!"

And they all played tag happily that morning until the school bell rang.

About the Author

Alastair G Mckenna is a schoolteacher, international traveler and avid children's book author, Alastair has a wealth of experience, spanning over 26 years in dealing with children from all continents. Alastair is a firm believer in the power of reading to children to infuse little ones with a love for reading.

Other Books by the Author